MAC'S SPORTS REPORT

RACKET RUMORS

Book design by Jake Nordby
Illustrations by Simon Rumble

Published in the United States by Jolly Fish Press, an imprint of North Star Editions, Inc.

First Edition
First Printing, 2018

Library of Congress Cataloging-in-Publication Data (pending)
978-1-63163-232-7 (paperback)
978-1-63163-231-0 (hardcover)

Jolly Fish Press
North Star Editions, Inc.
2297 Waters Drive
Mendota Heights, MN 55120
www.jollyfishpress.com

Printed in the United States of America

MAC'S SPORTS REPORT

RACKET RUMORS

BY KYLE JACKSON
ILLUSTRATED BY SIMON RUMBLE

PREDATORS OVERMATCH GULLS

by Mac McKenzie

This afternoon, Coyote Canyon's girls' tennis team (7–1) continued its impressive resurgence with a hard-fought, nail-biting road victory over Oceanview Middle School (5–3). The Predators' winning point came in the closing act of a long, tense afternoon. With all other individual matches decided, and each team having won three of them, only the first-ranked singles, or first singles, remained on the court. The top players' teammates surrounded the court, cheering.

Coyote Canyon's new first-singles player, Roe Danner, slammed one powerful backhand after another into the corners. Her worthy opponent from the Seagulls, Jane Rodriguez, scrambled to dampen Danner's heat. Ultimately, the Predators' star power proved too much for Oceanview's top player. Coyote Canyon once again relied on its new weapon at the top of the lineup to pull out a close match.

No Coyote Canyon team has reversed course so dramatically as the girls' tennis squad. And while every member of the team has made contributions, the arrival of new student Roe Danner has been essential to the team's success this season. Her stranglehold of the top spot in the Predators' lineup has pushed her teammates down a slot in the team's individual standings. Because of Roe's presence, each Predator is now consistently playing an opponent she has a chance to beat. This wasn't the case a year ago, when our Predators went 1–12, finishing last in the conference.

"Roe is a marvel," Coach Frankles said, describing her top player. "She just keeps coming, relentlessly, with those heavy backhands. She wears opponents down. We wouldn't be having the year we're having without her, that's for sure."

Danner was not available for a post-match interview.

CHAPTER 1

Scuttlebutt.

That's the word.

Stewart "Mac" McKenzie has been searching the archives of his brain for the perfect word the last several days. He couldn't find it until a moment ago. He had just rolled his wheelchair out of his social studies class and started heading toward his locker at the other end of the school when suddenly, there she was next to him: the one and only Roe Danner. She just happened to be making her way down the same hall as him at the same time.

Of course, Mac would love to do an interview. But Roe's not looking to have her story told—that much has been obvious by the way she's dodged him at the end of this season's tennis matches. As students' attention shifts to them—well, to *her*—the word Mac has been digging around for is finally right on the tip of his tongue. It's the best word he knows how to describe his Coyote Canyon classmates' behavior.

Scuttlebutt. He'd learned the word last year from Ms. Stark, his seventh-grade English teacher. Scuttlebutt is what you call the bucket of water sailors gather and tell stories around. Made-up stories. Far-fetched stories. Stories meant to entertain, not to report the truth. According to Ms. Stark, the word has a double meaning. Over the years, the word has come to mean not only the bucket of water around which the stories are told but also the *act* of telling the stories. When people make things up about others and then share the information like it's the truth, it's called scuttlebutt.

As a reporter, Mac hates scuttlebutt.

A less careful thinker or a less precise writer may have settled for *rumor-spreading* or *gossip* to describe the Coyote Canyon Middle School's student body's treatment of Roe Danner. Roe, the school's introverted tennis prodigy, enrolled only this fall and, by all accounts, has said barely a word to any other student. But Mac is nothing if not careful and precise. He's a firm believer in the dogged pursuit of facts and sticking to the story—the sports story, in his case. People love to hear stories spun and exaggerated. Mac likes novels and movies as much as anyone, but when it comes to real people, he sticks to the facts. In his mind, it's only fair.

Mac admires a lot about his fellow students. As Coyote Canyon's resident sports reporter, he has watched them push past hardship and achieve success. He has watched them support one another in defeat. And whether on championship or struggling teams, Mac's peers tend to be good teammates. They like each other and treat each other well. Mac tends to like many Predator athletes off the fields and courts as well. They are his close friends and his acquaintances, his fellow sports fans, and his enthusiastic readers. Sure, if one examined the entire student body, they would find, as Mac's mother might say, a rotten apple or two in the pile. But day in and day out, Mac likes to think the Predators are good to one other.

But. They do have a nasty habit—not unlike every other middle school student who's ever existed. Curious by nature, the Coyote Canyon student body just can't accept not knowing about something—or someone. They need to know what happened, how, and why. It's why they're such avid readers of his articles. In the absence of known facts, however, they make up their own. They attempt to do Mac's job, and they do it badly. Irresponsibly. Dangerously. Unfairly. They turn to scuttlebutt.

No one in Mac's time as reporter has ever been so enticing to these manufacturers and consumers of scuttlebutt as Roe Danner.

This is because no one knows anything about Roe. She

doesn't have a single friend at the school. She doesn't look anyone in the eye. No one's sure (if they're being honest) if she has raised her hand at any point during a class or given a presentation of any kind. If forced to work in a group, she listens attentively and does her part, but never contributes ideas out loud. Even during her tennis matches, which she nearly always wins, she never calls or corrects the score—something her opponents take advantage of at times, though she tends to dominate them so thoroughly they can't cheat their way to victory anyway.

It seems as if every Predator has a different theory about Roe Danner. Some people say Roe thinks she's too good to associate with the rest of the school. Others say she's simply shy. Some even theorize that Roe is part of the Witness Protection Program—that she or someone close to her did something so terrible or brave she now needs to pretend she's someone else. If she's hiding from dangerous people, students at Coyote Canyon explain, she wouldn't want to risk getting too close to anyone and accidentally revealing her secret.

Mac's reporting instincts tell him this is all silly. He has no idea why she keeps to herself, but she doesn't strike him as elitist or shy. *And, really, the Witness Protection*

Program? Mac laughs to himself. *It's way too far-fetched to be true.*

At first, everybody said these things quietly and behind Roe's back. But it's more than a month into the school year, and Roe hasn't shown any signs of letting her classmates in, and the scuttlebutt has gathered steam. When Roe shuffles through the halls, her classmates aren't so subtle in their pointing. Their voices aren't so soft and secretive. It's become common news that Roe Danner *is* the news, and no one knows the first thing about her.

Today, Mac travels the hall beside Roe Danner and feels his classmates' eyes on the both of them. The crowd parts down the middle, everyone's backs against the lockers as they watch Roe and Mac move through the center of the hall. Their whispers envelop him, and Mac wants all the more to make them stop.

Mac can't understand why Roe puts up with it all. Why doesn't she talk to anybody? If she doesn't want to make friends, why doesn't she at least tell people to mind their own business? That's what Mac would do.

As a reporter for *The Coyote Courier*, the school's newspaper, Mac is responsible for reporting on Coyote Canyon's sports stories. And right now, there is no bigger story than the girl shuffling next to him. Mac realizes then

how badly he wants to cover this story. To stop the rumors and set the story straight. If he reported on Roe, he'd make the story all about who she is on the court—the quick-footed champion with the most devastating two-handed backhand anyone has seen since Monica Seles' early years on the pro tour.

Unfortunately, no one seems to care about who Roe is on the court when she's such an intriguing mystery off it.

Scuttlebutt bounces off the walls like tennis balls backhanded by Roe herself. She continues walking, apparently unaffected by students' gossip. Mac is impressed, but he's not sure he can take much more of the outlandish, uninformed stories. He knows he needs to confront the rumors and tell her true story. Maybe then everyone will stop making things up.

CHAPTER 2

Mac isn't surprised to see Samira that afternoon as he arrives at the school's tennis courts. She's even more of a stickler than he is about showing up to watch warm-ups at the Predators' sporting events. "You can see if someone's ready to play by how they get loose," she once explained to Mac. "You can see if they're carrying themselves with confidence. Isn't the whole point of going to a game to see how people are going to perform under pressure? Why would you skip the part where you can get the inside scoop on what they're thinking, how they're moving, before the game even starts?" she continued in total Samira fashion.

There is a reason Mac and Samira are best friends, and it's not just their love of sports. It's also how they think about sports—their strategy. When it comes to sports at Coyote Canyon, Samira always has the stats, and Mac always has the story. They make a good pair.

Thanks to her bright-orange hijab, Samira's easy to spot at the bottom of the stands. Also, besides a few parents, she's the only fan watching the tennis match. Mac has always wondered why tennis fails to draw a crowd. Sure, at major professional tournaments, entire stadiums are full of people. But anywhere else, including Coyote Canyon, no one seems to want to watch. It's such an exciting, fast-paced game. And it's easy to follow too: players hit the ball back and forth until one of them can't get it over the net or land the ball within the court's boundaries. Mac can't imagine why no one shows up. Except for Samira, that is.

"You almost missed warm-ups," Samira says as Mac nears and settles into his usual spot. Samira doesn't look at him as she talks. Instead, she's watching Roe Danner. Just like Mac, Samira's focus never leaves the court.

Mac has just turned his attention to Roe's warm-up when Samira asks, "So?"

Mac waits, expecting Samira to say more. When she doesn't, he says, "So, what?"

"So . . . what do you think?" she nods toward Roe.

Mac turns back to Roe. She looks the same as always. Her short dark hair is pulled back into a couple braids, and, even though it's only warm-ups, sweat already dots her brown skin. As usual, her movements along the baseline are quick and balanced. Her opponent, Mim Lee from East River, is tall and slender. She hits a pretty heavy ball, Mac notices, but her feet are slower than Roe's. There's no way she can cover the court as well.

Mac is about to ask Samira what he's supposed to be looking for when he sees what has fascinated her.

"Um, why is Roe hitting a one-handed backhand?"

"That's what I want to know," Samira says.

Mac watches Roe hit another weak one-hander across the net to Mim. Her footwork is as confident as ever. She gets to the ball early, shifts her weight. But then she stabs at the tennis ball rather than following through.

Samira sighs. "Every one of her one-handed backhands just floats over the net. Like a plastic bag in the wind or something."

"What does that make her usual two-handed backhands?" Mac asks.

Samira thinks about it. "Like a speeding bullet?"

"Isn't that Superman—faster than a speeding bullet?"

"You put me on the spot. I couldn't think of anything better. The plastic-bag comparison was a good one, though. You can steal it for your article about this tennis match."

Mac smiles. There's nothing he loves more than bantering about sports with his best friend. When he turns back to the end of Roe's warm-up and watches her float another one-handed backhand to her opponent, he feels his smile fade.

Mac tries to think this through. Why would a tennis

star choose to hit soft one-handed backhands rather than devastating two-handed backhands that have been her best weapon all season? He can come up with only one explanation. "Maybe she's just working on the one-handed backhand during warm-ups. I bet she'll start hitting two-handers once the match starts."

Samira, who has continued to concentrate on the warm-up, sends a quick, skeptical look at Mac. "So, she's gonna play a match without ever getting her best shot ready?" she asks.

When warm-ups end, it's time to decide who will serve and from which side of the net. Roe approaches the net, spins her racket, and hands the tennis balls she has to her opponent. She retreats to the baseline to return serve.

"Moment of truth," Samira says.

Mim Lee is definitely skilled. Her first serve, to the deuce court, finds Roe's backhand. With one hand, Roe pushes the ball back to her opponent. The ball lands short in the court, and Mim pounces on it, smashing an inside-out winner past Roe, who has charged the net.

"So that's another problem," Samira says, shaking her head.

"What—that the girl she's playing against is good?"

"No, that Roe charged the net. Since when does she

return and volley? Usually, she just hangs out on the baseline and slams two-handed backhands past whoever she's playing."

Mac shrugs. "True. So she made a tactical error. Is that such a big deal?"

"Mac, buddy," Samira shakes her head. "You haven't been paying enough attention at tennis matches this year."

Mac scrunches his brow. "What does that mean? You know I watch carefully. How else am I going to write an accurate story?"

"Fine, so you watch carefully. But you haven't spent as much time on Court 1 as I have. You're always trying to give equal treatment to all the players out here. Because I'm not a reporter, I can stay with the talent."

"Okay. What am I missing?"

Samira pulls her gaze away from the court to look Mac in the eyes. "Simple. Roe Danner doesn't make 'tactical errors.' Ever. She has some kind of calculator in her brain, and she always seems to know what the percentage play is. She never beats herself."

Mac is about to say, "Everyone makes mistakes, Samira," when he catches himself. There is no Predator out there, except maybe himself, whose sports knowledge he trusts more than Samira's. Like Mac, she's a sports junkie.

She's always watching sports, reading about them, or arguing about them with anyone she can find (most often it's Mac). She knows what she's talking about.

Roe loses the first game, and she and her opponent switch sides of the net.

Mac watches Roe serve at love-all. It's the same unimpressive serve he's seen from her in the past. Roe's serve is the only part of her game that doesn't impress. She doesn't hit it very hard, and she doesn't put much spin on it either. Mac knows her serve is what's called a "get-me-in" serve. It doesn't help her at all, but it does get the point started. Usually, this is enough, since Roe wins nearly every battle from the baseline. Today, though, Roe doesn't hang back at the baseline after hitting her get-me-in serve. Instead, she follows the weak serve forward. Just like when she was returning, Roe is coming to the net during her service games.

Roe's opponent scalds a forehand by her before Roe even has time to twitch.

"I just don't get it. Why is Roe serving-and-volleying?" Samira asks.

Mac agrees—it doesn't make any sense. "You got me," he says.

Roe loses this game and then the next. She's down 0–3 in the first set, and Mac knows he should go watch the other singles and doubles matches Roe's teammates are waging. Otherwise, he won't be able to report on the overall performance of the team. But Mac can't tear his eyes away from the disaster unfolding in front of him.

When Mim Lee hits a winner down the line past Roe for the final point, Roe turns and heads back to the baseline. Mim has to call to her to let her know the match is over and that it's time to shake hands. With carnage strewn across the court, Roe Danner—tennis *prodigy* Roe Danner—loses two of three sets, 0–6, 0–6.

Mac knows his job of solving the mystery of Roe Danner, and ending all the rumors their classmates are spreading, has just gotten more difficult. Because if people like gossiping about a winning athlete, they *love* gossiping about a losing athlete. Especially one who doesn't seem to care.

"What are you going to write about the match, Mac?" Samira asks.

Mac can only shrug.

"Maybe you should start with how Roe's one-handed backhands floated over the net like plastic bags in the wind?" Samira cracks.

Mac smiles an empty smile at his friend. He's still in shock after watching the Predators' best player essentially forget how to play tennis. "I just might steal that from you. Because I have no idea how to write about what we just saw."

GIRLS' TENNIS CONTINUES STRONG SEASON

by Mac McKenzie

"Her one-handed backhands floated over the net like plastic bags in the wind." This was one observant spectator's review of the performance of Roe Danner this afternoon in a tennis match against East River's Mim Lee. To be sure, Lee came ready to play, and she made Danner pay for nearly every soft, short backhand. In the end, it was an ugly loss for the Predators' first-singles player.

Danner stole off the courts before she could be interviewed. Perhaps the best analysis of today's match is that she is developing a new shot that didn't quite work out.

Fortunately, many of Danner's teammates fared better against East River in the home team's 5–2 victory.

The scores:

Singles

- Roe Danner (CC) loses to Mim Lee (ER) 0–6, 0–6
- Blaire Gunderson (CC) defeats Anisa Johnson (ER) 6–4, 7–5
- Tina Tunney (CC) loses to Annie Benson (ER) 2–6, 6–7 (3–7)
- Divya Deo (CC) defeats

Insley Horchner (ER) 1–6, 7–6 (10–8), 6–1

Doubles

- Rebecca Besse/Maggie Ebert (CC) defeat Gregoria Jones/Maya Jordan (ER) 6–3, 6–2
- Lucie Hamzawala/LaTisha Adams (CC) defeat Sam Kim/CiCi Daniels (ER) 6–1, 6–0
- Evelyn Lillie/Alex Togramadjian (CC) defeat Blanch Sinds/Jennie Lot (ER) 6–3, 6–4

After this doubles domination, the home team's record improves to 8–1 in its most promising season anyone can recall. The optimistic fan can hope that a day in which Roe Danner's teammates picked her up, as she has done for them over the past month, will only buoy the squad as it moves closer to postseason play. The team will need a stronger showing from its top performer in the weeks ahead. Danner's stellar record provides reason for optimism.

CHAPTER 3

Just as Mac begins his eighth circle around the living room, he suddenly brings his chair to a halt. From right behind his shoulder, he hears his older sister's voice.

"Hey, big-time sportswriter boy. Remember the family rule? You wake her, you put her back to sleep." Cue Mac's younger sister, wailing in his older sister's arms: "*WAAAAAAAAA!*"

Usually, Mac sits on the couch when writing his articles. But when he has writer's block, he finds that circling the room helps spark his thoughts. Mac turns toward his older sister, Maggie. "Sorry, Mags," he says to her. Mac and Maggie are a few years apart and travel in different social circles (Mac loves sports and Maggie loves everything but). But despite their differences and almost constant bickering, Mac secretly feels close to his older sister. Everyone who knows them both says they look alike. They have the same brown hair and the same freckles on their cheeks.

Their younger sister, Nora, already has her siblings' dark hair. Eight months ago, when Nora arrived and shook up all their established routines, Mac wasn't so sure he

felt as close to her as he did to Maggie. The family rule became that whoever woke Nora had to put her back to sleep. Because Mac likes to finish his sports writing at night, Nora often becomes his responsibility. His loud key-punching and frequent circling of the room are often determined to be the reasons for Nora's late-night crying sessions. Sometimes, Mac pretends that he's frustrated with Nora, but he can't actually be mad. Once in his arms, she always settles back into sleep. Listening to her sweet breathing always reminds Mac of how good the world can be—especially when whatever Predator team he's currently covering isn't having its best season.

This past week, however, Nora has been waking up the family even more than usual. A couple days ago, when Mac went to check on her, she had a slight cough. Mac's parents assured him that it was just a small cold. But it's been two days and the cough only seems to be worse.

Maggie, who is currently bouncing the baby gently in her arms, doesn't seem too concerned. She and Mac watch Nora's eyes flutter. Her stomach rises and falls. Just like that, she's asleep again. After a moment of enjoying the silence, Maggie turns her attention to Mac. "How many times have you circled this room tonight?" she asks him.

Mac shrugs. He has no idea how many laps he's done.

Maggie holds up a finger meaning, *wait one second*, and leaves the room. When she returns, there's no baby in her arms.

Mac mouths "sorry" without making any noise. The McKenzie family has learned to hold full conversations in voices no louder than hushed tones.

"Aren't you past your deadline?" she barely whispers, looking at his computer screen. "It's 12:30. I mean, technically it's not even today anymore—it's tomorrow morning."

Mac sighs. "Yeah. I already submitted this story."

Maggie's eyes narrow. "But it—it's so short."

Mac winces because he knows she's right. This may be the worst article he's ever written. Not only is it short, as Maggie noticed, but it's also incomplete. It focuses on one player who lost instead of on the whole team, especially the players who won their individual matches.

This time around, Mac's staring at his computer screen, and his relentless circling had nothing to do with writer's block. It had to do with guilt. He knows he hasn't done justice to the match he was supposed to cover against East River.

For a moment, he's angry with Roe Danner. For being such a mystery and for somehow always finding ways to avoid being interviewed. She was so difficult to figure out that she distracted him from doing his job. But the anger doesn't last. He knows the incomplete story he wrote is no one's fault but his own. He says out loud, "I need to do better. I *will* do better."

Maggie chuckles quietly, once again amused at how seriously Mac takes his work. Unfortunately, his voice wakes up Nora once again. She begins her wailing again from two doors down: "*WAAAAAAAAA!*"

Maggie nudges Mac gently. "Your turn, bro," she says. "I'm going to bed."

Mac nods and rolls himself out of the room. He's sure he'll do a better job covering Roe Danner and the tennis team from now on. But if Nora has anything to say about it, he's going to have to do a better job on very little sleep.

CHAPTER 4

The journalism room, or the "bullpen" as Mac likes to call it, is as inviting as ever the next morning. It's not that the room is particularly pretty: it's dark, with windows along one side that look out at a brick wall five feet away, the result of a building expansion from more than a decade ago. It's messy too.

The truth is, not much work gets done in this room anymore, since most writers and editors have a laptop they can use elsewhere. Aside from Fridays (which is when everyone ends up in the room making final preparations for the newspaper to go live), the bullpen is quiet. The prior four days, Mac and the other reporters can use it as a meeting space. Every once in a while, they converge on the room to divvy out reporting assignments or to hash out ideas about the newspaper's online layout. Most reporters treat the room as an extension of their hall lockers—just a place to dump stuff. This includes a little bit of every-thing—notes, snacks, textbooks, and raincoats for when reporters' stories are outside and the weather turns.

Mac doesn't mind the meetings. He likes his fellow

reporters. But times like this—when the room is empty and quiet—are his favorite in the bullpen: there's plenty of space and quiet to think.

Since there's a good forty-five minutes before first period, Mac is one of what must be only a handful of people in the building. If he's not shooting baskets before school in the gym, he's often in the bullpen. It makes him feel productive to be up and at it when others are just waking up. At this time of day, before the sun's glare comes through the windows, Mac can look at his reflection in them and ask it how he's doing today—if he's measuring up to his own standards.

Today, the person he sees in the window's reflection seems out of sorts, a distorted version of himself. He turns away from the windows. Right now, he doesn't think he has the energy to be self-reflective. He's sure he doesn't have the energy to get any work done. At this moment, the bullpen offers him the chance to do something he's done very little of lately: sleep.

Mac beat himself up about his short article for the first part of the night, and then Nora kept him up for the rest of it. When he picked her up to comfort her last night, her eyes got droopy quickly enough, but every time he set her down in her crib, they burst open, followed by loud cries.

Once it became a pattern, Mac's dad stepped in, rubbing his eyes. He told Mac to go to bed, and then sat down to rock Nora. Mac didn't object. He's used to staying up late, but last night was a little *too* late, even for him.

Apparently, the night was too late for his dad too, who was practically falling asleep at the kitchen table while reading his newspaper this morning. Nora's cough had kept her—and him—up until dawn. When he told this to Mac's mom, her eyes clouded over with worry. She said she'd call the doctor to see if they could bring Nora in.

Now, in the dark, empty bullpen, Mac worries about his sister. *People get colds all the time*, he tells himself. But then he remembers how small and fragile she is, and the fear returns. He tries closing his eyes. After a few minutes, Mac feels a little calmer. Sleep pulls him away from the room and he has almost reached someplace warm and relaxing—

—when the bullpen's door bangs open and light from the hall fills Mac's eyes. Mac blinks.

"Mac! I hoped I'd find you in here."

Mac rubs his eyes and opens them, officially starting his day at school. Parker, another reporter for the school paper, is standing in front of him. Parker is tall and gangly. He has a mop of hair on top of his head, and he enters

rooms as if wearing rollerblades, always tripping into things and knocking stuff over. He's always moving—bobbing his head, loudly chewing gum. He looks to be in a particular rush this morning.

"Hey," Mac says groggily. "What's up?"

"Do you have your laptop on?" When Parker is excited or worked up, he has a habit of speaking quickly, like he's always catching his breath. The urgency in his voice helps wake Mac up a bit more.

"Always." Mac nods to the table next to him, where he set his laptop a few minutes ago.

"Great, can you go to the newspaper site?"

"Uh, okay." Mac turns so he's facing the computer, and clicks on the shortcut icon for the school's paper, opening the homepage. "What am I looking for?"

"Go to the sports section," Parker says. "To your article."

Mac navigates to the article, skimming over the title: "Girls' Tennis Continues Strong Season." At least the title honored the whole team and not just its puzzling first-singles player.

"See?" Parker says.

"What should I be seeing, Parker?"

"Well, I don't think your whole article uploaded—only the part about Roe Danner and then the team scores. I wanted to catch you before anyone else read it."

Guilt spreads through Mac's body once again. He breathes deeply, tries to exhale his shame. "Thanks, Parker, but that's it. That's all I wrote."

Parker looks stunned. Mac hopes this is because his friend sees him as a real pro, someone who covers events from an unbiased point of view and responsibly reports all of what happened.

Parker looks away. "Oh," he says. "Sorry. I mean, yeah, I'm sorry."

Mac breathes deeply again. "It's okay, Parker. I know I didn't get this one right."

Parker looks back at him. He starts nodding his head and chewing his gum loudly. "I mean, the title of the article isn't so bad, though I might have gone with something a little flashier. As for the article, maybe there's still time to add some details, you know, from the other matches, like besides Roe's match . . ."

"Probably not, but Parker, listen. I don't have anything more to add. I mean, I was just . . . just so caught up in Roe's match that I never made it to the other courts."

Parker grimaces. Then nods. He starts to speak but doesn't seem to know what he wants to say. After three attempts, he finally says, "Hey, what's that?" He points to Mac's laptop. They both lean in for a better look.

It's a comment under Mac's article.

From someone with the username DD4S.

Writing about Roe when she's winning makes sense— the girl's an amazing player. But she lost yesterday, and other Predators killed it. Why not write about them? One of the players came back from down a set to win! Why not write about the comeback? Seriously, is Mac covering Roe and no one else just because she's the best on the team? I guess that's one way to get readers . . .

Mac's face drops into his hands. Until this very moment, he has wanted to end the gossip surrounding Roe

Danner. As soon as people read this comment, he won't only be annoyed by the Roe Danner rumors—he'll be part of them. People will whisper his name throughout the halls all day. Maybe all week. Heck, maybe all year. That's how rumors work. They cause people to see what isn't there. Unchecked, they create a new reality.

Lifting his head out of his hands, Mac looks up at Parker. Maybe Parker can say something to ease Mac's mind. He can tell Mac that no one reads the comments, even though that's untrue, or that this will all blow over in no time.

Instead, Parker says, "Wait, Mac. You're not favoring Roe because she's the star of the team, are you? I mean I didn't think much of it, but you did walk through the halls together yesterday. Did you convince her to do an interview?" Parker starts nodding his head, not waiting for an answer. "I mean, I get it. Roe's a prodigy. Everyone's curious about her, so articles about her are sure to draw in more readers."

Mac's head drops into his hands again. He mutters, "Can't you see what's happening? You're falling for the rumor. I got distracted at one match—that's all. I'm not intentionally focusing on Roe."

Head still buried in his hands, he hears Parker's voice:

"Right. I'm sorry. Maybe no one will read the comment. Maybe this will all just blow over."

Hearing the words he hoped to hear, Mac now realizes how foolish they are. He doesn't believe them for a moment. He knows Parker doesn't either. The whole reason the school newspaper opened the comments feature to readers this year was so students would pay more attention. Stay more engaged. Care more about the stories. And it's worked. Lengthy conversations took place in the comments section to articles this fall. They've been mostly respectful, though there have been a few trolls out there looking to stir things up. Until this morning, Mac now realizes, Roe's name has somehow managed to stay out of the comments section. It's the one place nobody has gossiped about her.

Mac closes his eyes as tight as he can, trying to think. Because the truth is that instead of putting the Roe Danner rumor to bed, he has just given it a cup of coffee and turned on loud music. His article about yesterday's match has only made Roe more of a rumor target. None of this is going away quickly and quietly.

Mac finally looks up. He says to his friend, "I wish, Park. I wish." Just then another comment pops onto his computer screen, again from DD4S:

The more I think about it, the more uncool this is. What

if Mac's been covering only the best players all along? He did write an awful lot about Drew Borders in the basketball season. Maybe the whole paper is compromised. Some people work hard to win tennis matches. Shame on the Courier. *Get some ethics.*

Parker's voice: "Man, this DD4S isn't happy. I mean, maybe you should figure out who it is and talk to them before this thing explodes and everyone's talking about it."

Mac looks up at Parker, confused. "You mean, you don't know who wrote the comments?"

It's Parker's turn to look confused. "You do?"

According to his parents, Mac has been a reporter all his life—someone who has always noticed what's happening around him. Even as a toddler, they say, he picked up on things. He'd hear a car door slam outside and know who just got home. He'd know that his parents were trying to get him to nap when they'd dim the lights, and he'd tell them "No nap now." As a thirteen-year-old, Mac has to remind himself that his peers, even journalists like Parker, don't notice the clues that he does. They get caught up in the emotional story and don't let the observable facts lead them to a logical conclusion.

"Sure, Park," Mac says. "DD4S has to be Divya Deo, the tennis team's fourth-singles player. The one who came back and won her match after losing a set. I get why she's mad. You're right. I should find her."

With that, Mac snaps shut his laptop and heads for the halls. People have had issues with his writing before. After all, that's the price of being a sports reporter. But this time feels different—he didn't mean to, but instead of portraying the truth, he only fed the rumor mill around Roe. If people are already talking, and they likely are, he has to move fast.

CHAPTER 5

You might think it would be easy to find someone at a school. Everyone, after all, is on a schedule. And figuring out Divya Deo's schedule is the first thing Mac does this morning. But it's not so easy. Nothing as a reporter ever is.

Mac has to wait outside the office for ten minutes before Ms. Hepperin arrives, unlocks the door, and invites him in.

"How can I help you, my dear?" she says to Mac once she's propped the door open with a plastic stopper so he can follow her in.

"Hi, Ms. Hepperin. I'm looking for someone. A student. I need to find her for a story."

"Of course, my dear. And Mr. Williams has approved this, right? He's asked you to look up this student's whereabouts?"

Mr. Williams, a math teacher at the school, is the newspaper advisor. To put it mildly, he has chosen a hands-off approach to this position, which he was assigned in the fall. In his words to the staff before the school year began, "Listen. Many of you have been on the school paper for a year or two already. You don't need a newcomer telling you what to do. So let me know if I can help, but don't let me get in your way. Use each other as resources before you come to me." Translation: he gets a stipend for advising the newspaper, which is the only reason he agreed to do it, and he really doesn't have any interest in what teenagers write about their classmates. Mac hasn't seen him in the bullpen since that opening meeting.

All of this is too much to explain to Ms. Hepperin now. Instead, he says, "Of course, Ms. Hepperin. I just need to follow up on what happened at the tennis match yesterday. I didn't report enough of the details."

Perhaps Ms. Hepperin can see Mac's genuine sense of shame because after looking at him suspiciously for a moment, she asks him whose schedule he needs. She pulls up Divya on her computer and prints a copy of her schedule for him.

Mac pivots his chair in the cramped office. Ms. Hepperin says, "I can't say I've had many reporters ask for schedules before. This must be an important story."

"Yeah, well, we usually just ask around," Mac says. "Friends always know each other's schedules."

Ms. Hepperin cocks her head as she hands him the

copy of the schedule. "And what's different here, Mac? Certainly Ms. Deo has friends."

Mac takes a breath, then decides to answer honestly. "I guess my classmates are talking about each other enough these days. I didn't want to give them anything else to talk about."

Ms. Hepperin nods in understanding. Then, after thanking Ms. Hepperin and refusing a piece of candy from her oversized candy jar, Mac is out the door, waving good-bye with Divya's schedule in hand.

CHAPTER 6

Once Mac has Divya's schedule, his problem isn't solved. He still needs to find a way to talk to her without the whole school watching and gossiping about their conversation. And this needs to happen soon, before everyone's talking about her comments to his article.

At least he has first-period Journalism on his schedule. This really just means he has first period free to do whatever the newspaper needs from him. Right now, he determines, the newspaper needs him to find Divya Deo.

According to her schedule, she's going to be in Phys Ed first period. Mac hopes he'll get lucky and find her walking out to the soccer field without a huge crowd.

Mac is waiting outside in the courtyard between the athletics wing and the walking path to the sports fields. *If you're hoping to get lucky as a reporter*, he thinks, *you're already doomed*. As Ms. Hepperin pointed out, Divya has friends. What are the odds she would walk alone from the locker room to the soccer fields? Mac watches clusters of his classmates, four or five students at a time, come into view. The groups of friends are loud as they shuffle past.

Many students nod to him or say, "Hey, Mac. How's it going?" or "Are you in our gym class now, Mac?" While they're surprised to see him, Mac's pretty sure these students haven't yet read his article or Divya's comments. It's still early. His classmates tend to read and talk about the school newspaper at lunch or during passing time in the halls. He's grateful for the quiet before the storm. But it's unsettling, nodding good morning to all these people who could be talking about his article in a couple hours.

Mac has no idea why he thought he could sit in the courtyard unnoticed while his classmates strolled past him. Somehow, he'd imagined that Divya would show up first, and well ahead of any of their peers. In this fantasy, he would ask if he could talk to her on the way to the soccer field. He would apologize for not covering her match fairly. He would explain what had happened and promise it wouldn't happen again.

Now, with his classmates streaming by and greeting him, Mac recognizes how desperate he is to make this whole story go away. And desperation never works out for a reporter. A reporter's job is to notice the world as it is, not to make the world what he or she wants it to be. In other words: Mac, now that he's being honest with himself, knows there's no reason Divya will walk alone to Phys Ed.

There's no chance he will be able to talk to her without anyone else noticing.

Sure enough, Divya walks into the courtyard between Madeline Fields and Libby Bass, the three chatting away. And there's really no chance Mac can get Divya's attention without Madeline or Libby noticing.

Still, Mac decides to go for it. After all, he's not sure he'll ever find Divya more alone than this. And time is of the essence.

Mac clears his throat. "Uh, Divya?"

She looks surprised to see him. This happens a lot, Mac has noticed. People sometimes forget that when they comment on social media, the people who they write about are actually real. Mac knows it can be embarrassing to come face-to-face with the person you have written harshly about.

"Divya," he repeats. "Can we talk?"

Divya begins to speak but can't seem to get it out. She really does seem shocked to see him in the flesh. He wonders if maybe this really will all work out. If Mac could just talk to her now, maybe she'd help kill the story about him playing favorites.

But that's just his desperation talking again.

Divya doesn't say anything, but Libby does.

"Sorry, Mac—we're nearly late for class," she says. Mac is about to say that it will only take a minute. But before he has a chance, the three are already walking away, their backs to him.

Okay, Mac thinks to himself. *What's your next great idea?*

CHAPTER 7

Mac takes his time moving back through the courtyard to the school building. He considers his options.

He could respond to Divya's comments with his own. He could apologize for not fully covering the East River match. He could refute Divya's claims. He could even take a stand for himself and for the integrity of the newspaper. He could promise that neither he nor anyone on staff would ever set out to report a story in a biased way.

Responding to Divya's comments would make him feel better. It would give him a platform to not only defend his own reputation but also to support the journalism industry as a whole. Mac knows his school paper isn't the only news source attacked with unfair allegations these days. It's impossible to avoid talk about the supposed bias and corruption in mainstream media. Mac knows many of the allegations are ridiculous. People become journalists to find the truth. Anyone's capable of writing a bad article. But that doesn't mean everything reporters write should be mistrusted.

Mac would love to write all of this in the comments,

but he knows he can't. The *Courier* staff promised to stay out of the comments section. They wanted it to feel democratic—no voice louder than any other. And Mac's voice would be louder than Divya's or any other reader's. After all, his name is under the headline—a headline he got to write.

The reporting staff of the school's newspaper also knew that responding to comments might only make things worse. It would just bring more attention to the conversation and give more credibility to any opinion expressed.

So, even if it would feel good momentarily, Mac knows he can't respond to Divya's comments.

Mac could find Roe Danner and ask her to make it known somehow that he's not favoring her—that they haven't even talked before.

This idea, Mac knows, is even less plausible than responding in the comments.

To seek out someone who hadn't asked to be part of a story and ask them to deny it? Totally not fair. Also, Roe Danner doesn't talk to anyone, which was what made her the center of the rumors to begin with!

Before re-entering the school building, Mac comes up with what he believes is his best idea. A plan that will hopefully kill the rumors and give him a chance to cover more of the tennis team. He takes out his phone and texts Samira:

Hey. Do you have Divya's phone number?

Samira and Divya were lab partners last year in Earth science. That means they had to work together outside of school sometimes. If Samira hasn't read his article yet, she'll be confused, but she'll still send the number. They always help each other out, and often without question. That's what friends do.

Samira, as usual, gets back to him right away. And she's not confused either. The true friend and sports junky that she is, she's already read Mac's article. Along with Divya's phone number, she writes,

So, I hear you've compromised all of journalism.

Mac breathes deeply. That's the other thing friends are for—to give each other a hard time. He sends her an "unamused" emoji. Then he writes,

Thanks for the phone number, though.

She writes back,

No prob. Thanks for quoting me in your article. Best part of the whole thing.

Before re-entering the school, Mac texts Divya. It might be too late to undo the damage from his article, but he can at least try to give some of the other tennis

players the coverage they deserve. And since there are still rumors going around about his work in the *Courier*, Mac has a feeling his podcast would be the perfect way to do it. Whether Divya will agree to it is a different question—one that Mac likely won't have answered until *after* first period.

CHAPTER 8

When Mac gets back to the bullpen, Parker's still there. Mac remembers that his friend is working on a piece about funds for the student council. Since Parker hasn't reported on sports for as long as Mac has, he sometimes takes on non-sports topics, including student government. Mac sees Parker shaking his head in frustration and assumes he's having trouble moving forward with the story.

"Principal Hanks still unwilling to be interviewed?" Mac asks.

Parker's head snaps around so he's facing Mac. "Oh, hey, Mac," he says. "No—I mean, you're right, I still can't lock him down. He's avoiding the issue. But that's not what I was thinking about just now. Look." He points to his own laptop screen.

Mac sighs. He wishes his friends would stop telling him to look and just tell him what's bothering them. He's exhausted. He hasn't slept, he's caught up in his most difficult story to date, and soon he may be the center of school rumors.

Still, he rolls up to the table next to Parker and looks at his friend's laptop.

In the space under his article where it used to say *Comments (2)*, it now says *Comments (12)*.

"Twelve?" Mac asks. "There are seriously twelve comments? Already?"

Parker nods. "And not from Divya. From like eight different people. Let me show you the highlights."

Mac groans as Parker scrolls to the first comment after Divya's two. This one is from BBGun2004:

I second DD4S. Mac's done us wrong.

He scrolls to another comment, from BECS:

Yep. Not cool at all.

"They're not cutting me any slack, are they?" Mac mumbles.

"Nope," Parker says. "And, uh, I'm sorry, Mac, but it only gets worse."

Mac reads the final comment, from M-A-B-SO:

Like, no wonder newspapers are dying. The reporters are compromised. FAKE NEWS!

"Usually, there aren't so many comments this early in the day," Parker says. "What's got all these people reading about the tennis match before first period is even over?"

Mac closes his eyes and rubs them. "Some are from the tennis team. BBGun2004, that's Blaire Gunderson. She plays singles right behind Roe. She won yesterday, and I didn't mention her except in the stats. M-A-B-SO—that's got to be Maggie Ebert, first doubles with BECS, Rebecca Besse. They're all rallying around Divya. I mean, I understand why they're mad. But fake news? This is getting out of hand."

"Because of one bad—I mean, incomplete—article?" Parker asks.

"No, you're right: it *is* bad. But I don't think they're mad at me. Not really. They're having this great season, and no one shows up to their matches. Samira and I were the only students at the last match. And all anyone can talk about with the tennis team is Roe Danner, the new girl. I get it. That's hard. And the school paper sends someone to write about the team, and I go ahead and feature Roe, even when she lost but the team won. They were already feeling unappreciated, and I made it worse."

"Yeah, yeah," Parker says, leaning back in his chair. As usual, Parker craves the drama and isn't interested in rational explanation. Mac is guessing that's why he's so invested in the situation in the first place. "So what now?"

Again, Mac closes his eyes and rubs them. "Actually, I have a two-step plan."

The bullpen is silent for a moment. Mac looks up and Parker is waiting impatiently. "And those two steps are . . . ?"

Mac continues. "Right. Sorry. I'm tired, Park. Step one: help the team feel more appreciated. Step two: figure out who Roe Danner is and how to tell her story."

Parker nods a few times, thinking. "Okay. So I get step one. I mean, this is a newspaper. We really should highlight the tennis team's great season. I mean, I'm sure you'll do it better than anyone else could."

Mac can't help but smile.

"But why step two? I mean, if Roe's not talking to anyone, what's there to cover? And why do you need her story? Why not just report on the rest of the team?"

"People are already telling Roe's story. They're saying she doesn't care, or that she wants all the attention on her. I guess I don't buy it. None of these stories seem right. If she doesn't care about tennis, then how did she get so good? And does it really seem like she wants attention? I get the opposite sense—that she wishes nobody noticed her at all. I hate a false story, Park, especially when there's a real one out there to be found."

Parker chews his gum loudly, nodding. "But, Mac, I mean, don't take offense or anything, but maybe you're not the right person to follow Roe anymore? I mean, maybe you really are compromised here? If everyone thinks you're, like, playing favorites?"

Mac nods. "You're probably right. But I'm the sports reporter for girls' tennis, right? And this is a story on girls' tennis, isn't it? I've got a job to do. I just need to figure out how to do that job without making everything worse."

All day at school, Mac is on high alert, frequently look-ing around. Despite being more tired than he has ever felt before, he keeps his mind from drifting. He can't afford to get lost in thought and somehow end up rolling alongside Roe Danner like he did yesterday.

He checks his phone repeatedly throughout the day, hoping Divya has seen his text by now.

To avoid the rumors he knows are flooding the halls, he leaves each class well after the other students and arrives at his next one at the very last moment, right as teachers are beginning their lesson. He's a responsible student who has built up trust with his teachers, so they're willing to cut him some slack, giving him quizzical looks but saying nothing.

Mac skips lunch to avoid the crowd and texts Samira so that she doesn't wonder where he is. Then he heads to the bullpen and, after scarfing down an apple and a bag of crushed crackers he rescued from the depths of his backpack, he takes a twenty-five-minute nap before English class.

After school, Mac heads to football practice to see how the receivers look. It's a no-pads practice. The team has a light workout having just come off a win over the East River Raiders.

It feels good to put his mind to work on something other than the Roe Danner story. The afternoon is sunny, but it's a mild Southern California day in the mid-seventies. The breeze that comes off the ocean, out of sight but not far away, reminds him to take a deep breath. He remembers how much he enjoys his job, despite the events of the day.

His thoughts are interrupted by a voice he doesn't recognize.

"Hey, you're Mac, right?"

He looks behind him. Standing so close he can't believe he didn't hear her approaching, is a girl of average height and short dark hair.

It's Roe.

Mac sets down his tablet. "Yeah, that's right. I'm Mac. Hi, Roe."

"Hey," she says. It's not a friendly "hey" but it's not unfriendly either.

Just as Mac begins to say, "I've been wanting to talk to you," Roe interrupts him.

"I know it's not your fault, but I need you to stop writing about me. The tennis team's all mad at you, and if you keep it up, they'll probably be mad at me. And I can't have that. It's distracting."

Mac takes a moment to think. That pause is all Roe

needs. Before Mac knows what to say, she is walking briskly away.

Mac finds his voice. "Hey, Roe, can I ask you a few questions?"

She turns and gives him an exasperated—and maybe slightly amused—look. Then she shakes her head "no," picks up her pace, and is out of sight in no time.

CHAPTER 9

Sometimes, Mac is sure the world of sports has some sort of magic power. Because whenever life seems too complicated, when he has no idea what to do next, sports offers him a refuge—a way to escape what's troubling him.

As a fan, Mac can watch a game and completely lose contact with the world outside the field or court. When he's covering a game as a reporter, he becomes even more engrossed in the action. But his experiences as a fan and reporter can't even come close to how Mac feels when he's on a basketball court. He's able to do what he does best. He can't help but feel in the zone while shooting baskets and chasing after rebounds.

Mac plays for the Wizards on Wheels, one of the junior teams in SCOR's wheelchair basketball league (SCOR stands for Southern California Outreach and Recreation). Sometimes, the athletes he covers for the *Courier* will ask him if he plays any sports himself. He will always answer humbly: "Yeah, I play with the Wizards." But anyone who's seen Mac play knows his humility is misleading. Mac's coach says he is one of the best shooters in Southern

California. And there is no more prized skill in basketball than outside shooting. His killer shot racks up points for his team, and it also makes the opposing team defend more of the court, which opens the lane for his teammates. At thirteen, Mac's one of the youngest players on the team, but his skill and leadership abilities have earned him a captain's C on his jersey.

Today, Mac is relieved there's a captain's practice after school. Normally at captain's practice, the team does just that: practice. But this time, Mac and Ty Warren—Mac's co-captain and best friend on the team—arranged for the Wizards to scrimmage against another team. It's just what he needs to get his mind off the tennis team. And since the Wizards are currently between seasons, Mac is desperate for a chance to play.

Unsurprisingly, it doesn't take long for Mac to find his rhythm on the court once they start scrimmaging. During one possession, Ty drives the lane and, without fully stopping, whips a pass with his right hand over his left shoulder to Mac on the wing. He has the ball in and out of his shooting cradle in no time, and the ball arcs straight and true through the rim. Ty glides next to Mac on their way back to play defense and gives him a high five.

Ty feeds him the rock again on the next possession.

This time, two defenders race out to contest his shot. Ty dives to the basket behind the two defenders, and Mac finds him for a layup. They have the easy chemistry of two teammates who have played together for years—and they have. Ty's easily the best player Mac has ever shared the court with.

For two hours in a hot gym, everything is right in the world. Mac misses shots too, and he turns the ball over twice. He's playing against good players, some of them two or three years older than he is. Mac's skill more than makes up for the age difference, but sometimes he gets a bit too fancy and the defense makes him pay for it. Mac's never rattled by this. He knows that aggressive plays come with the risk of mistakes, and he makes a lot more positive plays than negative ones. There's a logic to the back-and-forth action of a basketball game. No problem is bigger than one possession at a time.

Mac is reminded of how much easier playing sports is than reporting on them. Playing sports is all about the moment. Reporting on sports is all about the bigger picture. It's about telling a story, with each game or practice representing a chapter in something larger.

Waiting outside for their parents to pick them up, Mac and Ty catch up. Since Ty goes to school at Mount Wilson, the two don't talk nearly enough outside of basketball season. When they do start playing ball again, their chemistry always comes back—on the court and off.

Mac is grateful to talk with someone who doesn't go to Coyote Canyon—it means he can discuss something other than Roe Danner. He's about to thank Ty for the much-needed break from school drama when Ty changes the subject.

"So, how's Roe Danner doing?" Ty asks.

Mac double takes and nearly chokes on air. Finally, he manages, "Wait. You know Roe Danner?"

Ty is clearly weirded out by Mac's reaction. "I mean, I don't *know* know her. I've never met her. But when an athlete has game like that, everyone's heard of her. I mean, how many tennis prodigies go to Coyote Canyon? Doesn't everybody know about Roe Danner?"

Mac smiles and shakes his head, grinning.

Ty says, "What are you grinning about?"

"A couple things. One: Roe Danner is literally the topic I wanted to get away from for one night. Second: I've surrounded myself with friends who are so sports-obsessed they somehow know about middle school players from other schools and they can't understand why anyone else wouldn't."

Ty smirks. "Well, yeah. Are you saying it's unreasonable to expect everyone our age to memorize USTA rankings in their spare time?"

Mac laughs. "Maybe just a little unreasonable, yeah."

"So, since we're on the topic, how's it possible that Roe lost a tennis match to a middle school player?"

"Back up a second," Mac tells him. "First, you need to tell me everything you know about Roe Danner." As much as Mac wanted to forget about Roe and the tennis team for an evening, now that Ty seems to have information, he can't stop himself from doing his job.

Ty agrees. He's used to Mac's non-stop reporting by now. "I know she played for Sea Breeze High School last year—even though she was in middle school. She played third singles on the varsity team as a seventh grader."

Mac raises his eyebrows. He didn't know that.

Ty continues. "There was this preseason article in a tennis magazine my family gets. The article wasn't only about her—it covered promising newcomers on all the regional varsity teams—but her picture was in there. So I started following box scores online. She was doing awesome for four matches or something like that. She was supposed to be this phenom. Her name was in those USTA ranked-players lists. According to the article, college scouts—Stanford, USC, you name it—were showing up at her matches. But then she just stopped playing. I didn't know if she was hurt or what. I was glad to see her name show up in your articles again this year, but I was surprised she was playing for a middle school team instead of varsity."

Mac nods. "You're right. She should be playing on a varsity team somewhere. I don't know why she's not."

"Well, why don't you ask her?" Ty says. "Isn't that your job?"

"That's the thing. Roe Danner doesn't talk to anyone. I can't even ask her friends about her because she doesn't have any. She just keeps to herself."

"She's not talking to *anyone*?"

"Right. No one." Mac thinks about this. "Except for me, I guess." Ty looks sufficiently confused, so Mac clarifies. "Just once. This afternoon, actually. She told me to stay away from her."

Ty cringes. "Well, there must be a story in there, right? I mean, you're not *that* bad. Pretty good shooter. Kinda smart. Fairly nice."

Mac rolls his eyes. "Oh, there's a story—if you consider a bad article followed by school drama a story. But that's beside the point."

"The point being . . . ?" Ty asks, trailing off.

Mac sighs. "That's what I'm trying to figure out."

"Well, you've got me intrigued. I'm going to have to get caught up tonight. I haven't read your bad article yet. Maybe I'll call you, just to let you know just how bad it is." Ty smirks at Mac. "And that's my ride," he says, pointing to his mom who just pulled up to the curb.

Mac gives his friend a playful push toward the car.

"You can hate on my articles anytime," Mac says, "so long as you keep feeding me the rock out there on the court."

CHAPTER 10

That night, Mac makes it to bed at a reasonable hour for the first time all week. He was initially wired after playing basketball. His brain kept replaying the events from the past two days: Roe's miserable one-handed backhands, the string of comments under his article, Roe telling him to back away from the story, and Ty's new slew of information. Apparently, Mac was lost in thought the entire car ride home.

When his dad pulled into the driveway, he finally asked Mac what was bothering him. "Just a lot going on at school," Mac told him. Then he remembered Nora's doctor's appointment. When Mac asked his dad about it, he reassured Mac that Nora was okay. The doctor said that she has a mild case of RSV, a virus that's common in babies and usually isn't serious. Nora might have cold symptoms for a week or two, and then she'll be fine.

Initially, Mac had to resist the urge to Google information about RSV. But an hour later, after a hot shower, Mac decides the doctor is right. *Nora will be fine*. The water not only washed away his dried sweat but also his racing thoughts, at least temporarily. He feels clean and comfortable for the first time in days. Lying in bed, his eyes close on their own, and he drifts toward sleep. That's when his phone buzzes and lights up.

Mac groans. He wants to ignore his phone. But he can't. The synapses in his brain are firing again, his curiosity awoken. He rolls to his right and grabs the phone from the nightstand.

A text message.

From Divya Deo.

hey mac. thanks for the note. yes i will do your podcast with you.

Mac's first thoughts: *Can I wait to get back to her until tomorrow? Can I please not think about this right now? Do I really need to devote a whole podcast to this?*

This month's podcast isn't supposed to happen for two weeks, when Coyote Canyon's fall teams begin play-offs—bumping it up to tomorrow will be a big change in the schedule. But Divya's answer is, after all, the one he wanted. Doing a live podcast with her will hopefully stop some of the rumors from getting in the way of the real story. And Mac knows the podcast can't wait. If he truly wants to catch up to the story, he has to work fast. Mac sighs, then texts back.

Great! Over lunch, then? Come to the journalism room at 11:30.

Mac is tempted to go to sleep, but he also needs to prepare for tomorrow's live podcast. It needs to go well. But then again, he could always write his questions in the morning. His sigh from a moment ago becomes a groan.

"*WAAAAAAAAA!*" Nora's cry breaks out from down the hall.

"That couldn't have been me," Mac grumbles. *Unless Nora has superpower hearing and can hear texting from across the house*, he thinks. Mac smiles at the thought and mutters, "Here I come, Nora." If he's going to be up thinking, he might as well have his favorite little sister (well, only little sister) in his arms.

Mac scoots toward the side of the bed, where his chair is waiting for him. Per the doctor's suggestion, Nora now has a humidifier near her crib to help her breathe. Mac's parents also gave her the medicine the doctor recommended. That means that after a few rounds through the house, Nora should be back to sleep. Hopefully, the same can be said for him.

THE MAC REPORT:
A MONTHLY LIVE SPORTS HUMAN-INTEREST PODCAST WITH MAC MCKENZIE

Today's Guest: Divya Deo, Coyote Canyon Middle School, Girls' Tennis

MAC: We're here with Divya Deo, recording from the newspaper bullpen at Coyote Canyon Middle School. Divya, welcome to The Mac Report.

DIVYA: Hey, Mac. Thanks for having me.

MAC: So, let's get right to it. Coyote Canyon's girls' tennis team is having an amazing season, with stellar performances by several star players. Today, let's focus on you, Divya. You play fourth singles for the Predators.

DIVYA: That's right.

MAC: And you're having a really good season! You're six and three on the year.

DIVYA: I should have won a couple more of those too. It was early in the year when I lost them. They were some of my first matches. I guess I hadn't, you know, gotten over my nerves or something.

MAC: Understandable. That's actually something I wanted to cover in this podcast: how you became such a solid presence in the lineup. You weren't in the lineup last year, were you?

DIVYA: No. I mean, I'd never played tennis before I went out for the team in sixth grade. Last year, I was a little better, but most girls on the team were a lot better than me. I started to really like the game, though. And if I was going to be at practice all the time, I didn't want to play exhibition matches anymore.

MAC: For our listening audience's benefit, tell us what an exhibition match is.

DIVYA: It's a match that doesn't count toward the team score. You play against someone from the other team who didn't make their lineup either. It's not terrible or anything. You still get to play. But I guess I thought last year, why not work in the offseason so I can play in matches that count toward the team score?

MAC: That makes sense. So how much work did you put in between last season and this one?

DIVYA: A lot. I took lessons three nights a week and played in tournaments nearly every other weekend.

RACKET RUMORS

MAC: That's pretty inspiring, Divya. I mean, you came back to the team this fall a whole new player.

DIVYA: I guess I did, yeah. In tennis, the players who play the most usually do the best. It's about muscle memory. You practice hitting a ton of tennis balls over the net and into the court so you can repeat that when you play a match.

MAC: And correct me if I'm wrong, but you don't play any other sports for Coyote Canyon, right? You're able to keep your sole focus on tennis.

DIVYA: Exactly. I mean, I was never really into sports or anything. In sixth grade, I swear I could hardly even touch a tennis ball with my racket, I was so uncoordinated. I just went out for the team to spend time with friends.

MAC: But then you actually started to like the game.

DIVYA: Yeah. It took me a while to admit it. I mean, no one in my family has really played sports before. My mom was actually surprised when I picked it up.

MAC: What does she think now?

DIVYA: Oh, she supports me. She paid for my lessons and tournaments and everything over the last year. That's a lot. Though I don't think she's thrilled that I'm spending so much time on the court. She always asks if I'm still planning to do math team and Quiz Bowl once the tennis season is over. She always thought I'd do robotics in the fall, like my older brother and sister did. And I had to drop out of this outside-of-school orchestra I was in. She wasn't happy about that.

MAC: So you're saying you've had to work really hard to be as good as you are at tennis? Including making some sacrifices?

DIVYA: Yeah, essentially.

MAC: Well, I for one am really impressed. I'm sure your tennis teammates and our listeners are too.

DIVYA: Thanks, Mac. We'd love if more students would come out and watch us play. Like you said, we're having a really good season.

MAC: When can they watch you play next, Divya?

DIVYA: We have a match this afternoon. We play Middlefield at 3:30.

MAC: Out on our courts, right? It's a home match?

DIVYA: Yes. We played a handful of away matches the

last few weeks, so we get to play here for the last few matches of the season. Our final match before playoffs is on Wednesday. We play our biggest rival, Sea Breeze.

MAC: I'll be there, and I hope those listening will be too. Thank you for your time and your story, Divya.

DIVYA: Thank you, Mac. I'm glad you thought of me.

MAC: That was Divya Deo, fourth singles for our eight-and-one girls' tennis team. Catch all of Mac's sports reports on this podcast channel or *The Mac Report* blog. This is Mac, and that's a wrap.

CHAPTER 11

That afternoon, Samira and Mac make their way to the tennis courts to watch the Middlefield match. "So," Samira says, "it sounds like the podcast went over well."

Mac nods. "Seems so. A few of the players thanked me for it when I saw them in the halls."

"Honestly, Mac, I wasn't so sure Divya Deo was worth a full podcast. She's having a good year, but she's at the bottom of the singles lineup."

Mac nods. "I wondered that going into the interview. But think of how much she's improved in such a short time. Next year, she could be one of the team's top players. I like covering the top athletes before they go big." Mac pauses. "Besides, the podcast was the perfect way to dispute the rumors. Now, no one can accuse the newspaper of playing favorites or intentionally ignoring parts of the story."

"You're taking yourself pretty seriously, Mac," Samira says. "I mean, you're not THAT important." The smile in her eyes tells Mac she's giving him a hard time. "Anyway," Samira continues, "Divya does have a great story. I don't remember her from last year's team, and now I know why.

Like you said on the show, she's a completely different player this year. Maybe that can become a new theme in your podcast: interviewing players who aren't stars in their sport but still contribute to the team."

Mac considers this. "Maybe. In the meantime, I'm going to see if I can write today's article without mentioning Roe Danner, except in the box score."

"And I won't spend all match next to Roe's court either," Samira says. "I want to see Divya play, now that I know how much she's worked on her game."

Mac and Samira are now close enough to the courts to see Roe warming up. Mac's jaw drops.

"Don't speak too soon, Samira," he says, gesturing ahead. "Looks like Court 1 may give you plenty to think about."

Samira sees what Mac is looking at, and her eyes widen. "You've got to be kidding me," she mumbles. "The Roe Danner mystery intensifies. Try not writing about her *today*, Mac."

GIRLS' TENNIS WINNING STREAK COMES TO AN END

by Mac McKenzie

The Coyote Canyon Predators' girls' tennis squad has had its best season in school history. Their 8–1 mark heading into yesterday's bout with the Middlefield Lions defied all expectations heading into match play this fall. Given the Predators' hot streak, the Lions did not pose much of a challenge. But they certainly brought one. After earning a 4–3 victory over the Predators, the Lions headed back to Middlefield with an improved 5–5 record.

Some Predators struggled less than others. In fact, the home team's doubles duos didn't seem daunted at all. They continued their recent dominance, winning all three doubles matches. Led by a first-doubles team of Rebecca Besse and Maggie Ebert, the three winning pairs served with precision and took over the net consistently.

Coyote Canyon's singles players had a longer afternoon. Second-singles player Blaire Gunderson lost a heartbreaker. Up a break in both sets, her opponent (Glinda O'Hearn) fought back to win both 6–4, 7–5. Third-singles player Tina

Tunney's match was just as competitive, but she, too, fell. Divya Deo at fourth singles was up a set before stepping on a tennis ball that rolled in front of her from another court, resulting in a sprained ankle. She was forced to retire in the second set, gifting Gabby Boone from Middlefield the match.

First-singles player Roe Danner failed to find her stride for the second match in a row. She repeated her recent strategy of coming to the net as often as possible, and looked sharper doing so. It was almost certainly her decision to play with a wooden racket—rather than the lighter, more powerful graphite racket she usually plays with—that cost her today. Danner couldn't hit the ball hard or accurately enough with her chosen racket, and Lauren Biandbadoga bested Danner 7–6 (3–7), 7–5. This gave Middlefield the fourth and winning point they needed for a big upset in the world of middle school tennis.

After the match, Coach Frankles didn't have any answers. "We had our opportunities today, that's for sure," she said, shaking her head in disbelief. "We'll just have to get back at it in practice. We have a big final match of the regular season coming up against Sea Breeze next week."

A big match, indeed. This loss to Middlefield

drops Coyote Canyon's record to 8–2, identical to Sea Breeze's own 8–2 mark. That means Wednesday's match will determine who gets the number-one seed for the playoffs beginning the following week. Good news for the Predators: the match is at home, which gives Coyote Canyon fans an opportunity to cheer their tennis team to victory.

CHAPTER 12

Parker nods his head slowly as he reads Mac's article. They're in the bullpen together the morning after the tennis team's loss to Middlefield. Though Parker's judgment of the article may not be as telling as Samira's or Ty's, Mac is still curious. Between his last article, worrying about Nora, and falling behind on sleep, Mac feels off his game. And that doesn't happen often.

Parker finally finishes. "This is a good article, Mac. I mean, it covers everything fairly. You say something about every match. I just can't get over the whole racket incident. I don't know much about tennis, but even I know players stopped using wood rackets like, what, twenty years ago?"

"More like thirty-five years," Mac says. "I looked into it. Even in the 1970s, lots of players used steel rackets instead. By the '80s, only a couple players—like Bjorn Borg and John McEnroe—were still playing with wood. Soon, it was all graphite. Borg tried to make a comeback and play with a wood racket in 1991, and it went about as well for him as it did for Roe yesterday. Using a wood racket against someone who's using a graphite racket is kind of like riding your bike on the freeway and hoping you can keep up with the cars."

Bobbing his head and chewing his gum, Parker says, "So weird. Why'd Roe do it?"

"Beats me. I don't know why she does anything. And she always leaves the courts before I can talk to her. The one time she approached me, it was to tell me to stay away from her. People usually have reasons for how they act. I want to help others understand where she's coming from, but how can I do that if she won't talk to me?"

"In the meantime," Parker says, "people will come to their own conclusions. Look."

Mac follows his friend's eyes to his laptop. There's a comment under his article. It's from BBGun2004 (also known as Blaire Gunderson):

I finally get it. It's not just the Courier. *It's Roe. She's a traitor. She's going to sabotage the match against Sea Breeze. That's where she was last year, and she transferred schools just so she could lose and make sure Sea Breeze beats us again this year.*

Right away, another comment appears, this one from LOLS:

Oh my gosh. That totally makes sense. Thanks BBGun2004. Now we finally know the truth.

And another, from JSQUARED:

Send her back to Sea Breeze!

Mac sighs. He knows Blaire's theory doesn't make any sense. Coyote Canyon is playing against Sea Breeze Middle School, and Roe had played for the high school team. Who leaves the varsity team at one school in order to sabotage a middle school match at another school? But that's the problem with rumors—they don't need to make any sense to spread. Mac is more interested in why Roe is playing for a middle school team in the first place.

Parker's voice interrupts Mac's thinking: "So you say BBGun2004 is Blaire Gunderson?"

"Yeah. It's got to be her. Plays second singles. She had to watch her super-talented teammate lose a match yesterday to someone she should have beat because she was using a wood racket. It's enough to frustrate anyone."

"But who are LOLS and JSQUARED?"

"I don't know," Mac concedes. "I don't know that it matters. I don't think they're on the tennis team—there's no one on the team with the initials JJ. So they're maybe friends of Blaire's. Or maybe they're just other students at school. No matter what, it's not good. Not for Roe, not for me, and not for the newspaper."

Mac doesn't see Roe that day in school, but he hears

her name every time he's in the halls. It seems to him that people's level of interest in Roe Danner at this point has a lot to do with how connected they are to the tennis team. If they have good friends on the team, they seem to say Roe's name with anger; if they don't have friends on the team, they say her name more with amusement. *Like, she really used a wood racket?*

Mac keeps on asking himself the same thing.

CHAPTER 13

Mac is on his way to the football field to gauge the team's progress implementing new offensive plays for tomorrow's game against Forrest View. He's almost to the field when his curiosity gets the better of him.

He turns toward the tennis courts. Mac wants to see what Roe looks like in practice. He also wants to see how the team is responding to yesterday's tough loss. *Will the team practice with confidence and joy? Or will yesterday's loss have created a rift between certain members?* And the most important question: *Has anyone convinced Roe to return to her graphite racket?* The sports reporter in Mac never stops questioning. He needs answers.

As Mac approaches the tennis courts, the first signs he sees through the chain-link fence surrounding them are positive. The players are gathered, sitting in bleachers that go largely unused during the team's matches. They're listening to Coach Frankles, who has enough resolve for all of them.

Coach Frankles ends the team meeting with encouraging words: "I believe in this team because we play for each other. We're in this together." She says it with such conviction that even Mac believes her. Though he suspects that it may take more than one inspiring speech to close the rift between players on the team.

Mac is proven right as Roe and Blaire, the best two players on the team, start hitting tennis balls back and forth on Court 1.

The problem isn't Blaire, at least not initially. She pounces on her first couple groundstrokes. She's quick to the ball, and her forehand looks particularly smooth today.

The problem is Roe Danner.

Mac wondered if anyone would talk her into using a better racket. But not only is the wood racket still in her hand, it's also in the wrong hand. She's playing left-handed.

Blaire notices and lets a weak shot of Roe's bounce softly to the fence behind her.

"Uh, what are you doing?" Blaire asks.

Roe doesn't say anything. Because she never says anything.

"Seriously, Roe," Blaire says. "Why are you playing left-handed? You're right-handed."

Silence spreads over the entire complex. Soon, everyone is looking at Court 1.

Coach Frankles notices and approaches the court.

"I don't get it," Blaire continues. "Is your right hand bothering you?"

Roe shakes her head. Then, she finally manages, "It's a long story."

Blaire says, "Fine." She sets her racket down, walks around the net, and sits cross-legged right in front of Roe. "I'm listening," she says.

Roe says, "Don't worry about it."

"But I'm very worried about it," Blaire says, frustrated. "I hate that I'm even thinking it, but we all know you played for Sea Breeze last year. And now you're playing with a ridiculous racket and with your off hand right before we play them this season."

"It has nothing to do with that," Roe says.

"So what does it have to do with? You're the best player in our conference and you've lost two matches in a row because of these weird decisions. If that's not sabotage, I don't know what is. What, is someone paying you to play this way?"

Roe looks up, like she's searching for an answer. "I hope so," she says.

"What's that supposed to mean?" Divya says from the bleachers. She must be resting her ankle today.

Mac has no idea where this is leading. And apparently,

Coach Frankles doesn't want to find out. "Okay, that's enough. I said we were playing for each other today, and here we are arguing. Practice is over. And no team practice tomorrow either. I don't care that we have a big match next week. Instead of Saturday's practice, we're going to get ice cream. Yes, you heard me. Ice cream."

Based on the athletes' surprised glances, Mac can guess that ice cream isn't normally part of Saturday practices.

Coach Frankles goes on. "What this group needs is a little relaxation and team bonding. A chance to remember that we're all in this together, and that as much as tennis matters, each of you matters more. Next week, we'll get back to hitting serves and groundstrokes. We'll need everyone's best for two good practices before Wednesday's match. But all of that can wait. First, some perspective."

Blaire looks like she wants to say something. Divya too. But neither speaks. Eventually, they nod their heads. They look at one another. Roe only looks down.

Coach Frankles continues, "Oh, and new team rule: everyone stays off social media this weekend. If you want to ask a teammate something, go to her house and knock on the door. Any questions?"

No one says anything.

Coach Frankles' eyes widen with surprise. "We'll meet

here on Saturday at noon and walk to get ice cream to-gether. I'll see each of you, armed with an open mind, then. Motivational speech ended."

Slowly, Blaire stands up, giving Roe one last wary glance. Tina Tunney picks up Blaire's racket and brings it to her. The courts are silent as the players gather their things and head back to the school.

As Blaire walks by Mac, she says, "Well, there's a story for you."

But Mac knows the story he wants to tell has yet to reveal itself. His focus is still on the courts. On Roe Danner, who hasn't moved.

When she finally does move, it's toward Coach Frankles. "I'm sorry, Coach. I'm trying my hardest. I swear."

Coach Frankles says, "I know you are, Roe. You're doing the best you can under the circumstances. Just make sure you're here at noon on Saturday, okay?"

Roe nods, though her eyes never rise to meet Coach Frankles'. Head down, Roe shuffles off the court and walks down the street. Mac watches her until she turns the corner, a block from school.

When Roe is out of sight, Mac heads to the tennis courts. He watches Coach Frankles pick up tennis balls three courts down. Mac did a feature on her last year, when she became the school's new tennis coach. He remembers how patient and poised she seemed then, even though her team wasn't very good. Her players respected her. Having witnessed her conversation with Roe just now, he's reminded of how much he respects her. He guesses that part of why Divya Deo and others worked so hard in the off-season is because they like their coach so much.

Mac heads toward her.

"Coach Frankles?" he says.

"Hey, Mac," she says without looking away from the pyramid of tennis balls she's building on the strings of the racket that she's holding.

"Can I ask you some questions, on the record?"

"Of course, Mac, and I'll try to answer as many as I can. I suspect there will be a lot I can't say."

Mac thinks about this. "So how about I keep it related to tennis, then? I'm going to assume you can't tell me what's going on with Roe Danner."

"Yes, let's keep it about tennis. Roe can speak for herself if and when she's ready."

"Okay."

Coach Frankles tips the racket so the pyramid of tennis balls rolls off the strings into the cart she's wheeling around with her.

She looks at Mac. "Alright, Mac. Shoot. How can I help?"

"Great. I'm wondering if there's any way you'll take Roe out of the lineup for Wednesday's match. I mean, if she comes back with that wood racket and keeps playing left-handed, isn't she a liability?"

"It's a fair question. And no, I won't take her out of the lineup. She's earned some leeway here. She was undefeated until this week. She's maybe the most talented player I've ever coached. She deserves to be in there."

Mac isn't sure how to respond to that.

After a brief pause, Coach continues, "You know, Mac, I listened to your podcast with Divya. You do such a great job as a reporter. And I loved that Divya got to share how much work she has put into her game. She deserves praise for that. Lots of these girls do. But it seems like no one gives credit to Roe for putting in that kind of time and work not just for one year but for several years. She's a natural athlete, and so people assume that everything comes easy for her. And maybe there's some truth in that. But a lot of it—a lot of why things look easy when she does them—is because she has played so much tennis that her body's more adept to the sport than other people's."

Mac considers this. He already knew it, he decides, but he wouldn't have been able to say it as clearly as Coach Frankles just did.

"Yeah, I get that. I'm not trying to give Roe less credit. I'm trying to tell this team's story as best I can."

"I appreciate that, Mac," Coach Frankles says.

"And the fact is," Mac continues, "Roe isn't playing like

your best player right now. Would you consider moving her down the lineup, maybe making her third singles and moving Blaire and Tina up to first and second singles?"

"That's another good question. But I can't do that for a couple reasons. First, what you're suggesting is technically against the rules. I can't replace a first-singles player with a second- or third-singles player who has a worse record. Roe is now seven and two. Even with her recent losses, that's still the best singles record on the team."

Mac nods. *Of course*, he thinks, *it's against the rules*.

Coach continues. "But even if I could get away with making the move, it wouldn't help the team. Blaire and Tina would need to play better players against Sea Breeze, and they'll already have their hands full against the people they're meant to play at second and third singles. See what I mean?"

"Yeah, I get it," Mac says. "So you're going to have to hope Roe figures things out, huh?"

"Yep. We're going to have to hope that she does."

"And what about the other players on the team? They seem pretty upset."

Coach Frankles smiles. "That's why I canceled practice for today and tomorrow. They all need a chance to see each other as more than teammates—to see each other as complex people who live complex lives. Everything will cool down over the weekend. Perspective usually does that. You know, Mac, you've been following this team pretty closely all week. Maybe you need a little perspective too? Family is always good for that. Spend some time with family."

Mac's mind immediately jumps to Nora, whose virus still hasn't gone away. He sighs. "Coach Frankles," he says, "perspective was exactly what I was trying to find here. Thanks for your time today."

Mac turns to leave. He doesn't see how rocking Nora back to sleep or fighting with Maggie would help the girls' tennis team. But then again, maybe taking a break from trying to help the team is part of Coach Frankles' point.

CHAPTER 14

Mac has no choice but to take Coach Frankles' advice. On Friday afternoon, he covers the football team's game against Forrest View. Then, that evening, he has another captain's practice with the Wizards. Afterward, Mac's and Ty's families decide to go for pie at their usual place— Baker's Batch.

Being out with the Warrens is just what Mac needs.

Ty's brother, Willy, is a senior in high school. He's a year older than Mac's sister Maggie, and tonight, like always, Maggie and Willy talk pretty much exclusively to each other. They talk about colleges, books, bands. They're both really smart, and Mac likes listening in on their conversations.

Mac's parents are at the other end of the table with Ty's parents. Over the years, they've all become good friends.

And of course Ty is seated right across from him.

They probably would be talking about the basketball game on the TV near the restaurant's entrance, but right now Nora is sitting in Ty's lap. Mac's little sister must not be as into sports as Mac because she somehow slept through

the Wizards' entire scrimmage. But thanks to the sleep, she now perks up.

Ty, with only an older brother in his family, can't get enough of Nora. He lifts her again and again. He asks her questions about what she finds most annoying about her brother. Ty spends much of dinner talking to Mac through Nora. Like: "Maybe someone we both know will pass the ball more often this season. A layup's a higher-percentage shot than a three-pointer. Yes, yes it is!" He only hands Nora off once, when she needs her diaper changed.

Mac loves all of this. After the week he's had, he's happy that he doesn't need to talk to anyone. That he can sit back and enjoy his family and friends without needing to come up with the right question or answer.

It doesn't last, this feeling of not needing to ask questions. With Mac, it never does.

Because being out with his family reminds him that he has never asked himself anything about Roe's family. And what did Coach Frankles say? That family is always good for finding perspective. And if Roe's acting strangely at school, doesn't that likely mean there's something happening at home?

Soon, Mac is pulling up the school directory on his phone. That's where he finds Roe's mother's name—Joan

Danner. Then, at Baker's Batch, sitting at a table with his family and one of his best friends, with a warm piece of strawberry pie sitting on the plate in front of him, Mac performs a Google search that sheds some light on the mysterious Roe Danner.

This week, Mac has learned not to expect to get any sleep. Tonight is no exception. Tomorrow, he's determined to finally get his interview with Roe Danner. He may not have the whole story yet, but he has some—and that's more than before. Mac just hopes it's enough to get Roe to open up. As the night goes on, he drifts between sleep and wakefulness, his mind whirring.

In the morning, Mac doesn't need to ask for a ride. The address for Roe Danner in the school directory indicates that she lives right by Coyote Canyon Middle School. So does Mac's family.

He heads out the front door. Four blocks later, he calls Roe Danner from in front of her house. In addition to providing her mom's name, the directory also provided Mac with Roe's home phone number.

Because she's been so elusive this fall, so hard to pin

down, Mac is startled when Roe answers the phone. "Hey Roe," he says, "It's Mac."

"Mac? Why are you . . . ?" By the sound of Roe's voice, she's startled too.

Mac attempts to answer her question. "I'm actually kind of in front of your house right now. I'd like to say that I don't usually do this sort of thing, but it wouldn't be true. I'm a sports reporter—I go where the story takes me."

"What?" Roe asks. Then the front door to her house opens, and Roe appears in the entrance. Mac hangs up his phone as he heads up the slight curve of her driveway.

Roe also hangs up. "There's no sports story here," she calls to him. "Just my life."

Mac steels himself. "Well, maybe the two overlap. Regardless, I've wanted to interview you all season, and here we are. Are you, uh, free to go for a stroll?"

She throws him a look that says, *You've got to be kidding me*.

But he's ready for this. Before she can make the next move—which might be to step back in the house and close the door—Mac says, "I looked up some of your mom's paintings online. I'm sure my laptop screen can't do them justice, but her work is amazing."

Roe's eyes grow wide until she narrows them. She

trudges down the front steps so she can say quietly to him, "I have a feeling I know where this is going, and I'm sorry, I don't want to have this conversation. I don't even know you, Mac."

Mac nods like he understands, but he doesn't— not really. *So what*, Mac thinks. *Her mom is a famous painter. It's no reason to close herself off from the world.* "I know you don't. Except I don't think your vow of silence is making life easier for you right now."

"I know how hard my life is, Mac. You don't need to tell me," Roe says.

"That's not what I meant," Mac says. When he's talking about sports, the words come easy for him. But this is new territory. He tries again. "Please, just once around the block. I promise, I want to help."

She gives him a hesitant look, and Mac is sure she's going to decline. But then, as usual, Roe surprises him. "Okay," she says, nodding her head once, slowly.

As soon as they start moving down Roe's driveway, Mac begins talking, not wanting to lose his small bit of momentum. "So, after practice yesterday, I looked up your address and number in the school directory. That's how I'm here. But I also found your mom's name in the directory too, and after a quick Google search and discovering that your mom is a well-regarded painter, I found this." Mac stops moving and holds up his phone for Roe to see.

On the screen is an image of an oil painting. Roe's mom painted a lot of portraits and landscapes, but out of the many paintings he scrolled through online, one stood out: a tennis player. The player is right up against the net, serving a one-handed backhand with his left arm. And he's using a wood racket. After seeing the painting, Mac couldn't get the player's face out of his head. Something about him seemed familiar. And after a little digging, Mac finally realized who it was.

Roe grabs the phone to get a better look. When she sees the painting, she quickly glances away. Her reaction confirms for Mac that he was right. There is a story here.

"So, my question," Mac says. "Is your mom a John McEnroe fan?"

Roe glances back at him, surprised. "That's all you want to ask me? All you came to talk about today?" Mac isn't sure how to answer. *Is he supposed to be asking her about something else?*

"Yes?" he says, unsure. Then he goes on. "It would all make sense. Your mom is a John McEnroe fan, and now she's putting all this pressure on you to play as well as him. So naturally, you try to play just like him—the serving and volleying, the wood racket, the attempt to play left-handed at Thursday's practice? You're trying to play tennis like John McEnroe."

Roe smiles, seeming relieved. She hands him back his phone. "That's not one of her well-known ones," she said. "I'm surprised you found it."

"I'm good at digging," Mac says, and he thinks he sees Roe smile.

"To answer your question," Roe says, "yes, she's a fan. And that's to put it mildly." Roe goes on to explain that her mother isn't just a remarkable painter whose work covers the walls of exhibits. Joan Danner is also a life-long believer that the sport of tennis is the truest art form there is. She believes that tennis's artistic beauty was best realized by the great John McEnroe, who dominated the game before graphite rackets allowed everyone to hit the ball way too hard. She mourns what she calls "The Lost Art of the Volley."

"I was even named after him," Roe says.

"That's pretty cool," Mac says. "Sometimes, people at school think I was named after the laptop. So, like, you definitely win."

Roe laughs then lets out a small sigh. "It feels good to talk about this, finally."

Mac jumps in, knowing that's his cue. "So why don't you tell everyone? If people understand that you're trying to play like a tennis legend, they'll respect you even more. I know you like your privacy, but if you open up, all the silly rumors will stop. And if this is about your mom putting too much pressure on you to play like McEnroe—or as good as McEnroe—then your teammates might be able to help. I know tons of athletes dealing with pressure from parents."

Roe stops walking. "You don't get it," she says. She looks up, like she's in a debate with herself and trying to figure out what to say next. "My mom's not putting pressure on me."

Mac stops too. *Then what is it?* he wants to ask. But he doesn't. Though the sun is bright, he thinks he can see tears welling in Roe's eyes.

"Mac, my mom is sick." She pauses, then takes a breath. "Really sick. She has ovarian cancer, and the doctors didn't catch it until late. She's been hospitalized for two months. She's had three surgeries in the last year. She's been through four rounds of chemo. She sleeps most of the time, when she's not vomiting."

Mac sucks in his breath—he thought Roe's mom was just a hovering sports parent. He never imagined something like this. He has a feeling that Roe's been waiting to tell

someone all of this for a long time, even if it's the last thing she wanted to do. He doesn't want to interrupt, but she's stopped talking, so he says, "I'm just—I'm so sorry, Roe."

She closes her eyes and nods. "Thanks," she manages. She gestures back toward her house, which they're close to again, since they've almost made a full loop. "This isn't my house, even. I'm staying with my aunt and uncle while my mom is in the hospital. Everything is so different. And I can't focus on normal things. I just don't care about the middle school stuff—making friends, winning at tennis, stopping the rumors. It's all pointless."

Mac tries to choose his words carefully before speaking. "Roe, I get that school and tennis matches don't matter to you right now, not when your mom is so sick, but then why even play on the tennis team? All your teammates count on you, and they don't know why you don't care about them."

Roe stiffens a little and stands up straighter. Mac is worried he's said too much, and that Roe will go back to her aunt's house, ending the interview. But for some reason, she doesn't. Instead, she sighs, then sits down on the curb and looks up at him.

They sit in silence for a few minutes. Mac has a hundred questions but none that he should ask. Thankfully, Roe speaks up again.

"Last weekend, right before I changed my playing style, my mom had a bad night. The doctors weren't sure she would wake up."

Mac searches for something to say. "I'm . . . I'm sorry. I honestly don't know what I'd do if that were my mom." Mac realizes just how true that is. If Nora having a slight virus makes him worry, he can't imagine what it would be like to have a family member be seriously sick.

Roe says, bitterly, "But it's not your mom. It's not anyone's mom but mine."

Mac nods.

"The thing is," Roe continues, "I've convinced a small part of myself that the only way to save my mother is to learn to play tennis like John McEnroe, a man who—" she puts up air quotes, assumingly quoting her mom "wielded his wood tennis racket like a paintbrush."

Roe explains to Mac that she doesn't know how long she'll have to learn to play like McEnroe. She might not have enough time to learn to charge the net and gracefully control points with surgical volleys as McEnroe did. She also admits that she's had no energy or desire to explain any of this to anyone. Winning matches or making friends haven't mattered to her in her grief, not for many months as her mother's health got worse and worse.

That's when Roe tells Mac everything else—the stuff

leading up to this past week. She says that last year, when they found out that her mom's cancer had spread, she left the Sea Breeze tennis team. She says she couldn't possibly care about a sport when her family was falling apart. So this year, her mom sent her to Coyote Canyon, since Roe's aunt lived close to the school, and encouraged her to play tennis again. It was so important to her mom that Roe picked the game back up. But Roe decided to set aside varsity and play on the middle school team, where she wouldn't need to take it so seriously.

When Roe has exhausted herself telling Mac all of this, he thanks her for sharing it all with him.

"And Roe," Mac says, "This can, of course, be all off the record. But I hope you'll consider letting me write a story on my blog about it."

She looks at him skeptically.

"No, I know. But hear me out," Mac says. "You're going through so much right now, so maybe what you need is more support. Coyote Canyon can feel judgmental, but it's also a pretty supportive place if you let people in. It's your call. I just think you'll have people like Blaire in your face more often if you don't give them a reason to understand where you're coming from."

Roe sighs. "I still don't think I can tell everyone. Telling you—though it feels good—is hard enough. But if you want to share the story . . ." She takes a deep breath. "Then I'm okay with it."

"Thanks, Roe. I promise to handle all of this with care, and I'll show you what I come up with before turning it in."

Roe nods slowly. "Okay," she says. "Thanks."

After a little while, Roe stands back up, and they head up the driveway to her front steps.

Mac has held himself back from saying many things this morning, but now that the interview is over, he lets one thought slip out. "Roe, I know this isn't my call. But I hope you'll think about playing right-handed against Sea Breeze. Keep your wood racket and your serving and volleying. But doesn't playing with your weaker hand actually make you play *less* like McEnroe? I mean, you can't volley as well with your left hand as you can your right, can you?"

Roe doesn't answer, and Mac knows there's nothing else he can say. He hopes he hasn't done more damage than good. He turns his chair and begins to roll away. Roe walks with him.

"Aren't you going into your house?" Mac asks.

"You've taken up my full morning," Roe says. "I have to get ice cream with the tennis team, remember?"

Mac nods. "That's right. Have fun."

Roe smirks before turning the opposite direction from him on the street. "Yeah. We'll see about that."

CHAPTER 15

It takes Mac all of Sunday to write his story about Roe. He knows he needs to get the tone, and every detail, just right.

By the middle of the day on Monday, everyone's talking about Roe. Mac hears some version of "Did you read about Roe?" repeatedly throughout the day. Mac keeps an eye out for Roe in the halls, but besides catching a quick glance of her before second period, he doesn't run into her. He knows she doesn't want the attention, and he hopes other people knowing about her mom doesn't feel too intrusive.

Mac acknowledges that none of this will help Roe's mom recover from ovarian cancer, but now that the rumors have been cleared away, now that the truth—the real story—is out there, at least the community feels more supportive of Roe. Now, people can stop making up reasons to be angry.

When no one from the tennis team comments under his article, Mac wonders if any of them have read it. Then he remembers Coach Frankles' new team rule about staying off social media. Maybe the combination of ice cream and talking face-to-face—instead of spreading rumors—can solve any problem.

Two days later, Mac is standing outside the tennis courts with Samira.

It's early. Warm-ups have just begun, and Mac and Samira are, as usual, the only two Coyote Canyon students in attendance.

"Well, she's still using that wood racket," Samira says.

"Now that I know why," Mac says, "I can't help but support her. I mean, I don't know if she can win with a wood racket. But playing for her mom—how can anyone not root for *that*?"

"And even if her mom weren't in the hospital, the return of the wood racket would make tennis a better game. I mean, when you can't hit the ball as hard, you have to do more with it. You have to play with more variety. That's more fun to watch—more fun even than watching Roe hit those amazing two-handed backhands."

"Do you think she can do it?" Mac asks.

"What?" Samira says. "Can she get everyone to use wood rackets again, because it makes for a more challenging game? Not likely."

"No—I mean, can she beat a good player like Rhonda Plank from Sea Breeze using a wood racket?" Other than the wood racket, Mac isn't sure how Roe plans to play today. In warm-ups, she's already tried out both her two-handed and one-handed backhands, some of them left-handed like at practice last week.

"I don't know, Mac. She does look more comfortable slicing that one-handed backhand today than she did last week."

"I suppose another question is whether she even cares if she wins."

"It does seem like she's more alert today, don't you think? Like she's paying attention?"

Mac agrees. "You know what? I think something good is going to happen today. I can feel it. Though it's too bad we'll be the only ones to watch it happen. Seriously, why don't more people come to tennis matches?"

Samira gives him a confused look. "But, I mean, we're not the only ones here. Look."

She points across the courts. Four Coyote Canyon students are watching through the chain-link fence. Then three more join them. Then four more.

In the next few minutes, more students show up. When perhaps fifty of them have arrived, they spread out to completely surround the tennis facility. Still more students come, filling in the gaps between fans.

"Mac," Samira says, "is everyone holding what I think they're holding?"

"That's right," says Parker, who suddenly appears beside Mac. "And some of us had to work hard to get our hands on one too." He twirls a wood racket in his hand, then nearly drops it. "Great idea, Mac."

Samira's eyes shoot to him. "You came up with this?"

Mac shrugs. "I may have gone in and made an addition, or should I say 'suggestion,' to Monday's post. But I didn't think people would actually do it. I didn't even think they'd see it. *You* didn't see it, and you're a Mac super fan."

Samira rolls her eyes. "Contrary to popular belief, I do things other than wait for edits to your posts. Anyway, I'm still curious. Where did everyone get these rackets?" She gestures to the students around her, wood rackets in hand.

Mac is curious too. He looks over to Parker, who is grinning.

Parker starts speed talking. "I mean, when you proposed the idea, I figured, how hard can it be to find a wood racket? Everyone's parents or grandparents ought to have one somewhere, right? That's where most people got theirs. But I come from a long line of tall, clumsy people. Apparently not even one of them ever stepped onto

a tennis court. Then I found this beauty"—he holds up a Jack Kramer Wilson model—"at Sammy's Used Sporting Goods."

Still stunned by the sight of more than fifty of his peers, Mac finally says, "We need to record this." He starts to pull out his tablet.

"No need," Parker says. "Mr. Williams is over there— see?" He points down the fence line.

"Since when does Mr. Williams show up for stories?" Mac asks. Their pretty-much-absent advisor usually showed little interest in the reporters' activity.

"I guess he wanted to see this," Parker says. "Apparently, he played high school tennis back in the day. He provided wood rackets for five or so kids today."

Samira cuts in. "But you guys, how'd you get the word out to so many people so fast? I can't imagine that this many people would notice a last-minute edit to your blog."

Parker answers her question. "A lot of people were looking for a way to support Roe. And also—" Parker leans in so only Mac and Samira could possibly hear him, "I may have started a rumor that John McEnroe is coming. Oh, and that he wants a picture with anyone who brought a wood racket. I swear, no one can spread a lie faster than the Coyote Canyon student body."

Mac laughs. "Gotta love the rumor mill," he says.

THE *FOUND* ART OF THE VOLLEY

By Mac McKenzie

Something out of the ordinary happened today on the Coyote Canyon tennis courts. The Predators' girls' tennis squad (8–2) began the day tied for first in the conference with this afternoon's opponent, the Sea Breeze Surfers. If anything, coming off a bad loss to Middlefield in which Coyote Canyon's singles players were swept, the Predators were underdogs in this one. The Surfers likely still don't know what hit them. This wasn't merely a win for the Coyote Canyon girls' tennis team. This was history in the making—a 7–0 victory that already feels like a tall tale.

As the teams concluded warm-ups, a massive contingency of Predator fans appeared, each wielding a wooden tennis racket. These rackets were a sign of support for first-singles player Roe Danner and her mother, Joan Danner, but it was also a sign of support for the version of tennis Joan Danner likes best— tennis that has more to do with skill and creativity than with power. Today, Predator fans cheered wildly, and their loudest cheers followed points won at the net. Encouraged by the fans' excitement, Coyote Canyon players looked for opportunities to approach the net and finish the point from there.

The Predators' under-appreciated doubles teams took control of points again and again, closing in on the net almost recklessly. They dispensed of their Sea Breeze opponents in record time. Second-, third-, and fourth-singles players Blaire Gunderson, Tina Tunney, and Divya Deo all dropped opening sets largely from the baseline before deciding to play to the fans as well. First-singles player Roe Danner closed the show, soundly defeating one of the best players in the conference, Rhonda Plank,

with a wooden racket. Roe forced Plank to scramble toward the net to track down impeccably plopped drop shots at other points, then drove volleys past Plank when she expected another drop shot. It is hard to believe that it has been only a week since Roe adopted this new aggressive style of play. Today, she channeled John McEnroe himself, carving up the court.

Fan support for Coyote Canyon tennis made all the difference today. The team responded to fans' enthusiasm with their most spirited victory to date. Make sure to join the team again next week, when our one-seeded Predators take on the ten-seeded Grapevines to open the playoffs.

CHAPTER 16

A week after the Sea Breeze match, Mac arrives at school as early as anyone's allowed in the building. He's in his very favorite spot (besides the basketball court)—the bullpen. After telling Roe Danner's story in a way that feels right and fair, Mac has had a few nights of better sleep. And miraculously, Nora has too. She's been waking up only once or so per night. Mac's parents think the virus might finally be nearing its end.

Now that they're both sleeping better, he actually kind of misses his extra-late nights with Nora. Last night, her crying woke him up, and he joined his mom in Nora's room just so he could be the one to rock her back to sleep. He's tired as he glances around the bullpen. But it's a good tired. The tired that comes from doing a good job, even if it meant skipping sleep for a week to do it.

Today, Mac loves his job. He loves that it's his responsibility to find the truth and tell the story. He looks into the window beside him, and instead of focusing on the view of the brick wall, he catches a faint reflection of himself. His grandmother likes to say, "If a person can look at herself in the mirror and be okay with what she sees, well, that person must be doing okay." Mac perfectly understands that now. His latest story was challenging—possibly his most involved yet. But at least now, with the truth out there, and until the next story comes around, he can take a break and enjoy the silence.

A voice interrupts his thoughts.

"Mac?"

He turns his chair. Roe Danner is standing in the doorway. Mac smiles, surprised.

"I hoped I'd find you here," Roe says. "I was talking to Samira yesterday, at lunch, and she said you come here some mornings."

Mac nods. "I do spend a lot of time in here."

Roe looks uncomfortable. Mac is suddenly aware the two of them have really only talked twice—once at any length. "I just wanted to say thanks. For everything this past week, I mean. I'm just . . . " her voice trails off as her gaze drops to the floor.

Mac waits.

Roe looks back up at him. "My mom had a good weekend. She was really alert. She's tired all the time, and, you know, this probably won't last. But it's good to laugh with her. And I told her about the Sea Breeze match. I read your article to her and showed her the video of all those fans with the wood rackets, and she loved it. I guess I don't know what's going to happen from here. But I'm glad I did what I did—learned to play like her hero—and I'm glad she knows about it. So, thank you."

Mac shakes his head. "You're the one who did the playing. I just wrote about it." Roe didn't need to thank him. She's the one dealing with tragedy.

"See you around?" Roe says.

"Yeah. See you around, Roe."

When she's gone, Mac looks back at the window. The sun is up and sending enough of a glare that Mac no longer sees his reflection.

No matter. He has work to do anyway—approximately a week's worth of English, social studies, and math. But first, he looks toward the large calendar on the wall that lists all of Coyote Canyon's sports events. *Who am I kidding*, Mac thinks, *I don't need a break.* The football team has a game tonight, and Mac will be there, ready to report.

ABOUT THE AUTHOR

Andy Hueller's books for young readers include *Dizzy Fantastic and Her Flying Bicycle* (also a play), *Skipping Stones at the Center of the Earth*, and *How I Got Rich Writing C Papers*. His life straddles Minnesota's Twin Cities. He teaches middle school and high school English in St. Paul, and his three-person, one-dog family resides in Minneapolis.

ABOUT THE ILLUSTRATOR

Simon Rumble lives in the United Kingdom. He has worked as an illustrator in the creative industry, worldwide, for over twenty years.

MAC'S SPORTS REPORT

BACK ON TRACK

BY KYLE JACKSON
ILLUSTRATED BY SIMON RUMBLE

MAC'S SPORTS REPORT

CONCUSSION COMEBACK

BY KYLE JACKSON
ILLUSTRATED BY SIMON RUMBLE

MAC'S SPORTS REPORT

SIDELINE PRESSURE

BY KYLE JACKSON
ILLUSTRATED BY SIMON RUMBLE

ALSO AVAILABLE

DON'T MISS MAC'S LATEST SPORTS SCOOPS

BY KYLE JACKSON
ILLUSTRATED BY SIMON RUMBLE

JOLLY FiSH PRESS

MAC'S SPORTS REPORT

BACK ON TRACK

BY KYLE JACKSON
ILLUSTRATED BY SIMON RUMBLE

Track and field season has arrived, and Mac is ready to report. Between last year's returning stars and standout newcomer Aleesha Ramos, the Predators are poised for an even better year at the state championships. That is, until practice ends, and meets begin. When the bleachers fill, Aleesha's sprinting is unremarkable. While the other sprinters warm up, Aleesha looks down. During races, she clips hurdles and loses speed. And afterward, she simply disappears. Mac is determined to find out why. Can Mac find out the cause behind the sprinter's poor performance? Or will the Predators lose their chance at a championship win?

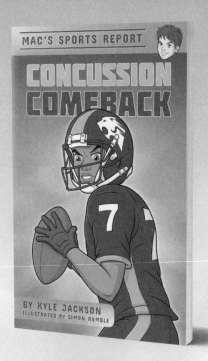

When the Predators' starting quarterback, Ryan Mitchell, gets sacked at the end of a game, Mac seems to be the only one concerned about the hit . . . at first. And even though Mac does not report his off-the-record talk with Ryan, Mac—and his reporting—has a lot to do with Ryan being sidelined with a concussion. When Ryan's starting spot gets bumped by a replacement, Ryan is furious with Mac. What will it take to get Ryan back in the game? And what will Mac do when he finds out?

The Predators are on a hot streak, but their star shooter is in a slump. Drew Borders isn't putting up the numbers, and no one—except Mac—wants to go on record as to why. It's obvious to Mac that Drew's overly critical and loud father, powerful attorney Larry Borders, is the root of the problem. When Drew is benched, and the sideline commentary from Mr. Borders doesn't stop, Mac decides to take matters into his own hands. Will the Predators miss out on the conference final with their sharpshooter riding the pine? And what happens when Mac uses his investigative reporting to call Mr. Borders' behavior into question?

...es, but ever since the arrival ...oner, there's one story he ...The introverted tennis prodigy may make herself known on the court, but off the court, she's a total mystery. And before long, Roe's playing starts sparking rumors too. Even though she's right-handed, she plays with her left. And instead of sticking to the baseline, she charges the net. She even replaces her state-of-the-art graphite racket with an old wooden one. It's up to Mac to discover the truth behind Roe's odd antics. If he can do that, he might be able to stop the rumors and help bring Roe the fan support she needs.

Stewart "Mac" McKenzie is THE sports expert at Coyote Canyon Middle School, and its best sports reporter. While he scores big on the court with his wheelchair basketball team, his love for all sports is equally epic. There isn't a stat he doesn't know, a player's name he doesn't recognize, a big game he hasn't seen.

MORE FROM MAC'S SPORTS REPORT

$7.99 US

ISBN: 978-1-63163-232-7

50799

9 781631 632327

JOLLY FISH PRESS

 www.facebook.com/JollyFishPress

@JollyFishPress

@JollyFishPress